Twins

Secret Messages

A sinister stranger

2
POWER

A mysterious burglar

A hidden code

A jewel robbery

Danger

**Pete Johnson** has been a film extra, a film critic for Radio 1, an English teacher and a journalist. However, his dream was always to be a writer. At the age of ten he wrote a fan letter to Dodie Smith, author of *The Hundred and One Dalmatians*, and they wrote to each other for many years. Dodie Smith was the first person to encourage him to be a writer.

He has written many books for children, as well as plays for the theatre and BBC Radio 4, and is a popular visitor to schools and libraries.

*Books by Pete Johnson*

THE COOL BOFFIN
THE EX-FILES
FAKING IT
THE HERO GAME

*For younger readers*

PIRATE BROTHER

# PETE JOHNSON

## Illustrations by Rowan Clifford

PUFFIN

## PUFFIN BOOKS

Published by the Penguin Group

Penguin Books Ltd, 80 Strand, London WC2R ORL, England

Penguin Group (USA) Inc., 375 Hudson Street, New York, New York 10014, USA

Penguin Group (Canada), 90 Eglinton Avenue East, Suite 700, Toronto, Ontario, Canada M4P 2Y3
(a division of Pearson Penguin Canada Inc.)

Penguin Ireland, 25 St Stephen's Green, Dublin 2, Ireland (a division of Penguin Books Ltd)

Penguin Group (Australia), 250 Camberwell Road, Camberwell, Victoria 3124, Australia
(a division of Pearson Australia Group Pty Ltd)

Penguin Books India Pvt Ltd, 11 Community Centre, Panchsheel Park, New Delhi – 110 017, India

Penguin Group (NZ), 67 Apollo Drive, Rosedale, North Shore 0632, Auckland 1310, New Zealand
(a division of Pearson New Zealand Ltd)

Penguin Books (South Africa) (Pty) Ltd, 24 Sturdee Avenue, Rosebank, Johannesburg 2196, South Africa

Penguin Books Ltd, Registered Offices: 80 Strand, London WC2R ORL, England

penguin.com

Published 2007

1

Text copyright © Pete Johnson, 2007
Illustrations copyright © Rowan Clifford, 2007
All rights reserved

The moral right of the author and illustrator has been asserted

Set in Bembo by Palimpsest Book Production Limited,
Grangemouth, Stirlingshire
Made and printed in England by Clays Ltd, St Ives plc

British Library Cataloguing in Publication Data
A CIP catalogue record for this book is available from the British Library

ISBN: 978-0-141-31998-8

# Contents

# A Disappearing Sister

In the middle of the night, Sam woke with a jump. What on earth was that loud buzzing noise? It sounded like a bad-tempered wasp. Well, how dare it start rampaging around his room now? Talk about cheek!

He slid his head out from under the covers. At once the buzzing stopped. But then, to his complete amazement, he heard the voice of his twin sister, Ella, in his head. 'Sam, I'm trapped on the cliffs! Help me!'

He jumped up in bed and reached for his bedside light. Instantly, his room fell completely silent.

He must have been dreaming. Dreams can fool you sometimes. Hanging around when you think you're completely awake.

He was about to switch off the light again when he remembered how scared Ella had sounded. Most of the time Sam didn't like his sister at all, but he supposed he'd better just check she was all right. He'd creep into her room, see her sleeping peacefully and forget the whole thing.

He opened his bedroom door very carefully. He really didn't want to disturb

Uncle Mike, who was even grumpier at night. Then he tiptoed into Ella's room.

She wasn't there!

'Ella,' he hissed, just in case she was hiding under the bed or had fallen asleep in the wardrobe. He was starting to get scared. What was going on? Had Ella really just sent him a message?

Ages ago, when Ella and Sam had liked each other, they used to pretend they could hear each other's thoughts. It was just a silly game of make-believe at first. But they played it so often, it actually started to work.

Once Sam had been ill in bed and couldn't go to a party. But Ella had gone and kept sending him little 'messages' so he wouldn't feel left out. He'd suddenly hear her voice in his right ear telling him what was happening. And if he thought hard he could send messages back to her as well. It was so incredible!

But they hadn't practised anything like that for ages and ages.

Tonight, though, had Ella desperately tried to send him one more message?

But why would she be out on the cliffs now? It didn't make any sense. Unless . . . well, she had been sleepwalking a lot lately. Had she been sleepwalking tonight? A shiver ran right through him. Suddenly he knew he had to get to her as quickly as possible.

He hurriedly got dressed and then tiptoed down the first flight of stairs. His uncle and aunt ran a hotel called the Jolly Roger and he was now on the guests' floor. He was struck by the eerie stillness. Not a sound to be heard from any of the rooms.

Then Sam reached the hallway. He hated its musty smell, which swirled round you as soon as you stepped into this miserable little hotel. He was amazed anyone ever stayed here.

He unlatched the front door, slipped out and then closed it again with what he hoped was a soft click. A sudden breeze blew in with the strong scent of the sea. Some nights in the winter he used to open his window and listen to the waves furiously throwing themselves against the cliffs. But now it was April and the sea was much calmer, rising and falling on to the beach with a heavy sigh. Tonight, it seemed to be whispering something too: 'Hurry up, hurry up.'

'All right, I'm hurrying,' Sam whispered back. One of the few good things about living here was that the sea was straight across the road.

And soon he was scrambling on to the steep, chalky cliffs. He wasn't as surefooted as he liked to pretend. But luckily it was a clear night, with a bright moon.

A seagull suddenly dived above his head with a loud scream. It made him jump. Then he looked down. His stomach twisted in horror. Just ahead of him he could make out a shape. And it was lying very still.

## Secret Messages

Sam crouched down. Yes, it was his sister. She was on the cliffs just as her message had said. And she didn't seem to be moving. 'Ella,' he whispered, his heart pounding furiously.

Her eyes shot open. Sam sprang back in surprise. 'You took your time,' she said. 'I've been sending you messages for hours.'

'I'm so very sorry,' replied Sam

sarcastically, his concern for his sister melting right away. 'Just what are you doing out here anyway?'

'I would have thought that was obvious,' she replied, in that prim little voice he so hated. Then for the first time he noticed the two bags beside her.

'Oh, you're running away!' he exclaimed. 'Well, thanks for telling me.'

'Would you have cared?' she muttered.

'Not in the slightest,' he snapped back. 'But I'd still have liked to know.'

'Well, you know now.' Then she added, 'I was just taking a last look at the only thing I shall miss from here —' she nodded at the sea, '— when I slipped and fell . . . and as I didn't especially want to lie here all night I tried sending

you a message, just like we used to –
remember?'

'Oh, I remember all right.' Then he
murmured, 'That was before you got all
stuck up.' He was shaking a little, but
he really hated the way she looked
down on him; she never used to – but
she'd changed so much lately. Now
she'd turned into a total show-off.
And no brother wants a sister like
that.

A red flush began to creep over Ella's
face. 'I wish you'd stop saying I'm stuck
up,' she hissed, 'because I'm not.'

'You so are.'

They'd stopped liking each other
months and months ago, and it seemed
nothing could make them be friends
again, not even the shocking news, last

October, that their parents had been killed in a terrible train accident.

Then they'd had to leave their home in London and be handed over to Mum's sister, Aunt Joy, and her new husband, Uncle Mike. Going to live in a hotel in a small seaside town called Little Brampton sounded as if it might be fun. But it really wasn't, especially when they were given a huge list of chores to do every single day.

Sam knew his sister hated living at the Jolly Roger as much as he did. But he never tried to cheer her up – he wasn't exactly sure why. Perhaps he was just too busy being miserable himself. So most of the time he and his sister totally ignored each other.

He could even remember the last time

he'd spoken to her. It was four whole days ago, on the beach. The police were chasing a suspected jewel robber out on the cliffs. He and Ella had joined the large crowd watching the police capture him. Then Sam had turned and said to Ella, 'Now, that was exciting.'

'Yes, it really was,' she replied and looked as if she wanted to say something else. Actually, Sam did too. But neither of them could think of a single thing to say and finally they just walked off in different directions.

Ella looked at Sam. 'Are you going to help me up then?' she asked.

'Got nothing better to do,' he replied.

Once on her feet, Ella winced with pain. She gulped hard. 'Right, I'll carry

on running away now. Goodbye.' She
began to hobble off in the opposite
direction.

'Where are you going?' Sam
demanded.

'Not exactly sure. I've saved up money
from my tips – I've got nearly twenty
pounds now – so I'll just see what turns
up.' She took a few more slow, painful
steps.

*A slug could move faster than her*,
thought Sam. He really couldn't let her
go blundering off like that. He yelled,
'Ella, you can't leave now!'

She quickly turned round. 'Why
not?'

He struggled to explain. In the end he
just said, 'Because if you go, Uncle Mike
will make me do all your work as well.'

Ella didn't answer, she just shook her head in a disappointed sort of way and staggered off again.

Sam knew he should say something else. But what? It was so long since he'd chatted to his sister. In the end he cried, 'Before you go, I want to see if I can send you a message – like we used to!'

She turned round again and shrugged. 'All right.'

Sam struggled to remember how they used to do this.

'First you've got to clear your mind,' called Ella.

'I know,' he snapped, though actually he'd forgotten.

'Then start thinking about me,' went on Ella.

'Yes, teacher.' She was eight minutes older than him, but she always acted as if it was eight years. She'd boss him around all day if she could. Maybe he should just let her go. But in the end he closed his eyes, concentrating fiercely now, and tried again. He began picturing Ella in his head. She didn't look anything like him, with her straight brown hair, small green eyes and millions of freckles, which he knew she hated . . .

His nose started to itch: this was often a sign that things were about to happen. All at once that buzzing noise started up again. How could he have forgotten that was their little signal which meant you were making contact?

He sent her his first message: 'Ella, are you receiving me?'

'Loud and clear,' flashed the voice in his right ear.

A tingle of excitement shot through him. He sent her a second message – somehow it was easier talking to her like this: 'I think you should wait until your ankle heals before you run away.'

To his surprise, she replied, 'I agree. I shall run away tomorrow instead.'

And a few minutes later, with Sam walking beside her and carrying both her bags, she stumbled back to the hotel.

Sam put the bags down as quietly as he could outside her bedroom door. 'You can give me my tip later,' he whispered.

Without another word he went back to his bedroom. His right ear felt very hot. He remembered that had happened before when he and Ella had been passing messages to each other.

He'd just got into bed when he heard the buzzing sound again. And then Ella said, 'Thanks for rescuing me. I really didn't think you'd bother, so it was a good surprise. Bye.'

## Sam's Amazing Discovery

Ella didn't run away the following night. Her ankle was still painful and she decided to wait until it had healed. Three days later, though, her ankle was fine again and she thought it really was time to go.

She planned it all out on the way back from school. As usual she was on her own. She and Sam never walked back together.

Aunt Joy was waiting for her in the hallway of the Jolly Roger. She was a very thin woman with a long, pinched face, and lips which hardly moved when she spoke. This made her voice sound really dull and flat.

'Hello, Aunt Joy,' said Ella.

'You're very late,' she replied. 'Come into the kitchen at once.' There, she hurled a mop and bucket at Ella. 'Your first job tonight is to clean the floor.'

'Can't I just change out of my school uniform first?' asked Ella.

'No time,' boomed a voice right behind her. 'You can put this apron on.' Uncle Mike was a very large man who could somehow move extremely quietly. Often he'd just pop up out of nowhere.

When Ella and Sam first came to stay

at the Jolly Roger he'd smile at them – well, he'd bare his teeth. Uncle Mike thought they were wealthy orphans. When he found out they weren't, his whole attitude changed instantly.

Ella would hear him whispering, 'Those brats are eating us out of house and home.' Then he decided to save money by getting rid of the staff and letting the 'brats' take over their duties. Now she and Sam actually had rotas up in their bedrooms, listing all the jobs they had to do each day.

No, Ella wouldn't miss anything about living here, except the sea and maybe Sam, a teeny bit. Since that night on the cliffs they at least smiled at each other.

She decided to send Sam a message while she was cleaning the kitchen floor.

According to the rota, he was working away already in another part of the hotel.

She thought of nothing for a moment, and then began imagining Sam: his very blue eyes, the shiny dark hair that flopped over his forehead, his cheeky grin. She'd just reached his long skinny legs when that buzzing noise exploded in her right ear.

'Hi, Sam, what are you doing?' she asked.

He replied, 'I'm doing my top hobby in the entire world, hoovering the stairs. You'd never think I could hear you over all this noise but I can, loud and clear.'

Ella gave a little shiver of delight. This was like their own, totally private, totally free phone line. And they could chat away for as long as they wanted. How cool was that? She said, 'I'm running away tonight – and I thought you'd like to know. I'll tell you where I'm going.'

He sounded stunned by this news. 'Tonight? As soon as that?' Then he groaned. 'You won't believe this – some guests have arrived already and I've got to carry all their bags up as the lift's broken again. Don't go, though, Ella, stay online . . .'

And then Sam started giving her a little commentary on what he was doing. 'I've got to carry Mr and Mrs Evans's suitcases upstairs, and they're huge. The cases, that is, not Mr and Mrs Evans. And kind Uncle Mike hasn't even offered to carry one. No, he's just marched into his office and slammed the door. Well, here goes.'

A few moments later Sam was back online. But his voice sounded strange and muffled as he asked, 'Ella, do you want to see something truly incredible?'

'Yes,' she replied at once.

'Well, go into reception right now and you really will, but,' he added quickly, 'you must stay online.'

Ella dashed out of the kitchen and into reception. Two people were staring up at the stairs, pop-eyed with amazement. Then Ella gave a little squeal of shock too.

For there was Sam, an enormous suitcase in each hand, jumping up those stairs two at a time. And when he got to the top he actually lifted the suitcases right above his head and started twirling them!

Poor Mrs Evans collapsed into a chair and was now breathing very hard. 'I couldn't even lift those cases they were so heavy, and yet that young boy . . .' She began to breathe even harder.

Sam waved a suitcase at Ella.

Ella stammered, 'B-But how? How?'

'How yourself?' grinned Sam. Then he added, 'Isn't it fantastic?'

# The Phantom Fork Bender

'It was as if I'd turned into the strongest boy in the world,' cried Sam.

Three hours had passed since Sam had lifted up two extremely heavy suitcases as if they were feathers – and, not surprisingly, he was still talking about it.

He and Ella had managed to slip out of the hotel for a few minutes. They were walking along the beach together. She said, 'I thought poor Mrs Evans was going to pass out with shock.'

'I know,' chuckled Sam. 'She kept worrying that I'd strain myself. But those cases were as light as anything. Well, they were while I stayed online with you. But the second we stopped talking together, they were agonizingly heavy again.'

Then Sam tried picking up a giant rock. He couldn't budge it at all. But as soon as he and Ella went online, he could lift it right up into the air.

'Look at that,' he cried triumphantly. 'The moment I'm online with you I become mega strong, if not mega, mega strong.'

Then Ella wanted to have a go.

'I'm not at all sure it will work for you,' he said.

But it did. In fact, Ella raised the rock even higher than Sam had.

'You had to do it, didn't you?' he snarled.

'Do what?' she asked.

'Show off,' he shouted.

Ella hated, *hated*, HATED it when Sam said she showed off because it was totally untrue. Yes, all right, at their old school she had been top in every subject. But that wasn't her fault, was it? She didn't even try especially hard. It just happened. And she did think Sam might have been pleased for her. But he wasn't. In fact, that's when he started ignoring her. She'd call his name and he'd just turn away. It was so stupid. But in the end she had no choice but to ignore him right back.

She really liked being friendly with Sam again, though, so when he lifted the rock once more and declared, 'That's much higher than you managed,' she didn't argue (even though it wasn't true).

Back in the kitchen they had to wash up after the guests' supper. But no one was about so Sam whispered, 'I've got an idea. But we'll need to get online first.'

Once they were buzzing, a mad gleam danced in his eyes as he grabbed a fork. And in the blink of an eye he had bent the fork's handle right back. 'There's magic in my fingers,' he cried triumphantly. Then he seized a second fork. That was swiftly twisted right back too. 'Twisting forks is my new hobby,' he declared.

'Very good, but you'd better stop now,' said Ella.

'Why?' he demanded.

He was reaching for another fork when they heard Uncle Mike boom, 'Hope those brats have cleared everything away! I'm absolutely exhausted.'

Ella and Sam started madly bunging plates away, just as Uncle Mike and Aunt Joy marched into the kitchen.

'Haven't you finished tidying up yet?' demanded Uncle Mike. 'What have you been doing?'

'Well, the thing is,' said Sam, 'we've been really puzzled by something.'

'What . . . ?' began Uncle Mike. Then

he stopped and took in the two bent forks on the table. He let out a bellow, like a mad bull. This was followed by a screech of surprise from Aunt Joy.

Ella had to look away or she knew she'd burst out laughing. But Sam managed to ask with a straight face, 'Do you think we've got a phantom fork bender in the hotel?'

Ella's shoulders began to shake. No, she mustn't laugh. She really mustn't.

'When I find out which guest has done this . . .' roared Uncle Mike, his tiny eyes glinting with fury. 'Well, no one makes a fool out of me.'

He went on, 'And you two aren't going to bed until this kitchen is spick and span.'

'And make sure everything is set up

for breakfast tomorrow,' added Aunt Joy, who was hunched right behind him.

That took the twins another half an hour. But when they'd finished, Sam was still grinning from ear to ear. Ella couldn't remember the last time she'd seen him look so happy. She said quietly, 'Sam, we must keep our special powers secret from Uncle Mike.'

'Why?' he demanded.

'If he found out he'd probably sell us to a circus or something.'

'That's true,' agreed Sam at once.

'And actually, I think it's best if no one knows except us.'

'Yes, all right,' said Sam, 'it'll be more fun if it's just us two.' Then he asked, 'Are you still running away tonight then?'

She hesitated for just a moment. 'No, I think I'll wait another day or two.'

He grinned at her again. 'Been great here tonight, hasn't it?'

She agreed it had. But Ella also thought they should be using their amazing new powers for better things, other than bending forks.

And the very next day she had a brilliant idea.

# Digging for Treasure

Ella's brilliant idea came from the local paper. Splashed right across the front page was a story about a local man who'd found a Roman coin buried in one of the cliff sides. It was a rare bronze coin with the Emperor Nero's face on it, worth hundreds, if not thousands, of pounds.

The paper said that other Roman coins might also be out there and people were already frantically searching. Lots of them were using metal detectors.

Ella began to get very excited. Suppose she searched for the coins too? Only, she would be online with Sam while she did this, meaning she'd be extra strong and able to dig deeper than anyone else.

She couldn't wait to tell Sam her plan. But he wasn't very interested at first. 'Who cares about some mouldy old coins?' he asked.

'But you're forgetting,' cried Ella, 'how much those coins could be worth – maybe thousands of pounds!' Now she had his full attention all right. She went on wildly, 'Just think what we could do with all that money! We wouldn't need to live with our rotten relations for a start. We could move out. We'd probably have to pay someone to look in on us for half an hour now and again as we're not adults. But the rest of the time we could do what we wanted, live where we wanted . . .'

'Got ya,' cried Sam eagerly. 'Let's go find a rare coin right now.'

But there was no chance of getting away that day. They were kept busy by Uncle Mike and Aunt Joy every second.

The following day was no better.

Finally, they decided not to go back to the hotel after school finished. Instead, they made straight for the cliffs where the Roman coin had been found. At last they could start treasure seeking.

It had rained for hours but now the air smelt wonderfully fresh and there was a brilliant blue sky. Sam scrunched up his eyes and pictured Ella in his mind. Then his nose started to itch as if he was about to sneeze. He was about to go online all right. Next came the familiar buzzing . . .

'Hi, Sam,' said Ella excitedly into his right ear. 'I can't wait to get started.'

Two men were already digging away furiously. 'They're keen,' said Sam.

'Let's find somewhere right away from them,' cried Ella. 'We don't want anyone to see us digging in the magic way.'

They discovered a secluded spot on the cliffs. 'We'll start here,' declared Ella. She produced the spade she had bought from her running away money.

'I'll dig if you like,' said Sam.

'No, I'll do it,' said Ella firmly. Sam

didn't argue – it was her spade, after all – but he was disappointed. Still, it was a laugh seeing her dig so incredibly quickly. In fact, it was like watching a speeded-up film of someone, with soil and stones flying everywhere. All the time Ella was digging, she chatted to him online. 'This is brilliant fun,' she cried. 'And I'm not tired at all.'

Sam noticed the two men walking away from the cliffs. They looked dejected. They obviously hadn't found anything. But then neither had Sam or Ella.

'Perhaps we should try somewhere else,' said Sam.

But then she hissed excitedly into his right ear. 'I think I've found something.'

'Yes?'

'You won't believe this . . .'

'Tell me.'

'It's a glasses case.'

'What!' he exclaimed.

Ella handed the case to him. He took out a pair of gold-rimmed glasses. 'They're massive and so thick,' he said. 'They must belong to someone with very bad eyesight. But what on earth are they doing buried out here?'

Ella didn't answer. Instead she squeaked, 'I've found something else.'

'What is it this time, a hearing aid?'

'No, it's a coin,' she cried excitedly, scooping it up. 'And I think it's a very old one.'

'Let's have a look then. Yeah, that looks dead ancient all right,' he cried, as he took a green coin, caked in mud, from her.

'Wow and double wow!' he exclaimed. 'Do you realize we're probably the first people to touch this coin for thousands of years? And we've found it – well, you did.'

'Couldn't have done it without you,' said Ella.

'That's true,' he agreed.

Back at the hotel they got a right earbashing from Uncle Mike. 'How dare you arrive back so late from school? I had to take some cases up the stairs myself.'

'And you know he's got a bad back,' cut in Aunt Joy, 'just as I've had this nasty cold for five years.' Her voice rose. 'And look at your school uniforms – all filthy. Whatever have you two been doing?'

Sam winked at Ella. To his slight surprise she winked right back.

In the kitchen they ran some water over the coin they'd found. The green colour on the coin started dissolving away and they discovered it was actually silver. On one side there was the profile of a man with cropped hair.

'That's a Roman emperor for sure,' said Sam. 'And that new coin they found was only bronze; this is a silver one – it could be worth millions.'

'We mustn't let Uncle Mike or Aunt Joy find it,' said Ella.

And at that moment Uncle Mike suddenly shouted, 'You two haven't got time to talk, you know!'

Ella dropped the coin in shock. Luckily Uncle Mike didn't notice, as he stomped up and down the kitchen issuing his orders.

'Phew,' said Sam afterwards. 'If he'd found that . . .'

Later Ella happened to glance at that day's edition of the local paper in reception. The discovery of the rare Roman coin was still front-page news. And, the paper said, Professor Forbes, the well-known local archaeologist, agreed that other valuable coins could be in the same area.

The professor was usually a very private man. But he was so excited by what might be found that he was inviting people to contact him with their discoveries.

Below was his email address. But, in fact, Ella knew exactly where the professor lived because a girl in her class lived in the same road.

And on Saturday afternoon she and Sam managed to sneak off to Professor Forbes's home. It was right at the end of the road. The garden was bright with daffodils and it looked like a happy house. Ella was sure the professor would be friendly and see them.

# We're Going
# to Be Rich

Ella rang the doorbell. They both
waited. 'I can hear footsteps,'
whispered Sam.

Bolts were drawn. A face appeared in
the gap. It was a woman with huge,
bulging eyes and a sharp, suspicious nose.
She somehow didn't fit such a friendly-
looking house.

'Hello,' said Ella politely. 'Sorry to
disturb you, but we found something out

on the cliffs and we'd like Professor Forbes to look at it.'

'I'll make sure he sees it.' And the woman put out her hand to take it.

'No,' cried Sam at once. 'We want to see Professor Forbes ourselves.'

'Well, I'm sure he won't have the time,' snapped the woman, 'he's such a busy man — but I'll check.'

Then she closed the door in their faces.

'She needs a lesson in manners,' said Sam angrily.

Ella gave him a friendly pat on the shoulder. *Sam gets mad so easily*, she thought.

'Don't worry about her. I'm sure Professor Forbes will see us,' said Ella. 'He's probably really curious about what we've found.'

And Ella was right. The woman returned and announced that Professor Forbes could spare them two minutes only. 'And make sure you wipe your feet,' she barked at them.

'I always do,' muttered Sam. 'I don't need to be told by you.'

*Oh dear*, thought Ella, *he's getting into one of his stroppy moods; that's when he could say the maddest things.*

They passed through a dingy hall and were led into a large, high room. The curtains were half-drawn already and a fire crackled in the fireplace, even though it was a warm day. Sunk in a chair in front of the fire was Professor Forbes. He looked even older than his picture in the paper. He was wearing tinted dark glasses and had a small white moustache.

'Good day, children,' he said in a high, quavery voice.

'Hello, mate,' replied Sam.

Ella blushed with embarrassment.

But the professor just motioned to them to sit on a couch opposite him. Then he said, 'I have some men searching for coins out on the cliffs. I think they saw you yesterday.'

'That's right,' said Sam. 'And we believe we've found something dead valuable, as well.'

'But how thrilling,' murmured the professor quietly. 'May I see this discovery?'

'Of course you can, mate,' said Sam. He turned to Ella. She dug in her pocket, then got up and proudly handed the Roman coin over to the professor.

He took out a magnifying glass and studied the coin. It was so gloomy in there Ella was amazed he could see it properly, although the fire did send little flickers of light over them.

'Is this all you found?' he asked.

'Yes,' said Sam at once.

Ella, who'd been feeling extremely shy, piped up, 'Well, apart from some old glasses.'

Professor Forbes's hand shook slightly. 'They weren't gold-rimmed spectacles, were they?'

'That's right,' replied Ella.

He looked up. 'Why, that's marvellous news.'

'You're not telling us those specs belonged to a Roman emperor?' cried Sam.

The professor smiled. 'Actually, they belong to me.'

Sam and Ella gaped at him in amazement.

'A few days ago,' he explained, 'we had a burglary here. Some money was taken as well as a few other things – and the burglar also ran off with my glasses.'

'A short-sighted burglar then,' grinned Sam.

Professor Forbes smiled back at him. 'Of course my glasses were no good to him. But his fingerprints were all over them so he had to hide them away somewhere where they wouldn't be found.'

'So he buried them out on the cliffs,' cried Ella.

'Exactly, my dear.' He lowered his voice a little. 'I'm afraid my eyes give me a great deal of trouble, which is why I daren't face the light. I have other glasses, of course, but those were my special ones. I'm so grateful to you both – do you have them with you by any chance?'

'They're in my bedroom, actually . . .' began Ella.

'Well, they're safe. That's splendid,' he said. He called out, 'Mrs Saunders,' and just as if she'd been listening at the door she appeared at once. 'We haven't been very good hosts. I'm sure my young visitors would like some refreshment. How about some orange juice?'

'You can throw in a few biscuits too

if you like, Mrs Saunders,' Sam called after her.

She quickly returned and banged down a tray bearing two glasses of weak orange juice and two very dry biscuits.

Professor Forbes was so thrilled at his spectacles turning up that he seemed to have forgotten all about the Roman coin, until Ella politely reminded him.

'Yes, yes,' he said, his eyes gleaming. 'This is a most exciting discovery.'

Ella and Sam stared at each other, their hearts pounding furiously.

'But before I tell you exactly how much this find is worth I need a second opinion. Now, by chance, I have a leading expert visiting me this evening: Sir Giles Westbury. I would like him to examine it – that is, if I'm allowed to keep your coin for tonight.'

'Of course,' said Ella at once.

'Just make sure you give us a receipt for it,' cut in Sam.

Ella blushed again. But Professor Forbes just nodded at Sam and said, 'You will go far, young man. Of course you should have a receipt for such an important find.'

He scribbled something on a piece of paper and gave it to Sam, who declared, 'That'll do nicely.' Then Sam said, a little too casually, 'And here's my card.' He'd made some cards at school featuring his name and address, and was extremely proud of them.

Professor Forbes chatted to them for a few more minutes. He was as nice as

Ella had hoped, full of questions about what it was like living in a hotel and where their rooms actually were. It was just a shame Mrs Saunders suddenly started hoovering right outside the door. Clearly she thought it was time they left. So Ella got to her feet.

Professor Forbes stumbled to his feet too. He wasn't very much taller than Sam. 'Come and see me tomorrow morning, when I should have some good news for you. And don't worry, I shall look after your coin. If you could also remember to bring my glasses with you?'

'Oh, of course we will,' said Ella, smiling at him.

He smiled back. 'Exciting times lie ahead for you both.'

★

Back on the seafront Sam shouted to a flock of seagulls, 'We're going to be rich!' and he and Ella laughed for a long time.

Finally, Ella said, 'I suppose we ought to go back now.' Immediately, all the fun and excitement of the day vanished.

'We're so late,' said Sam gloomily, 'they'll be going crazy.'

Then Ella said, 'Do you suppose if we went online we could run back really fast? Shall we find out?'

He nodded.

They closed their eyes and tried to concentrate. But it was just impossible on such a busy, bustling Saturday afternoon, so they walked on a bit until they came to an old footpath leading to

the park. They slipped down there. It
was deserted.

'Peace at last,' said Ella, and they got
online very quickly.

'Right, let's see how fast we can go,'
said Sam.

But Ella cried out, 'No, stop!'

'Don't boss me around,' he began
sulkily.

'Just listen,' Ella shouted.

Then Sam heard it as well.

It was a dog whimpering.

'He might be badly hurt,' said Ella.
'We've got to find him.'

They raced about, whistling for the
dog, but there was no sign of it
anywhere. By now they'd walked all
along the footpath.

'We'll be at the park soon,' began Ella.

But then Sam yelled, 'Look!' so loudly, he made her jump.

And there, tied to the fence post, was a small white terrier.

# Saving Patch

S am immediately charged over to the dog.

'No, don't rush at him,' urged Ella.

But Sam was already crouched down and patting the animal. It was shivering and looked very weak.

'Do you think it's just been left here?' asked Ella, stroking the dog too.

'Oh, it's been abandoned all right,' said Sam.

'And it's just skin and bone as well,' gasped Ella. 'Poor thing.'

Sam whispered to it, 'Don't worry, we'll look after you now.' The dog weakly thumped its tail. 'There, he likes me already,' cried Sam. 'And I love that little black patch over your right ear . . . I think that's dead cool.' Then he looked up at Ella. 'We'll have to take Patch back with us.'

'But they'd never let us keep him,' she replied at once.

'They need never know; we'll smuggle him in, then keep him in my room –'

'But he needs looking after,' interrupted Ella.

'I can do that,' said Sam promptly.

'But he's not well. We've got to take him to the vet.'

Sam muttered to himself, 'I've always, always wanted a dog.'

'So have I,' said Ella. 'But we can't –'

'No, all right,' he replied, springing up. 'We could go to that vet who came into our school. She seemed all right.'

Very gently, very carefully, Ella picked up the dog. 'I think Patch knows we're helping him. He keeps licking me.'

'He's probably just thirsty,' replied Sam.

When they reached the surgery the receptionist told them the vet was in the middle of an operation and really couldn't be disturbed. Instead, someone who didn't look much older than eighteen or nineteen appeared. Sam and Ella quickly told him what had happened and he immediately started examining the dog.

'Poor boy,' he murmured. 'You've been very neglected, haven't you?'

'How could anyone just dump a dog like that?' asked Ella.

'I'm afraid people do all the time,' the boy replied. 'He's not very old, so he might have been given as a present and then one day the owner decided they just didn't want him any more.'

'That's so cruel,' murmured Ella. 'I wish we could help him get strong again.'

The boy said he would personally look after Patch now and even take the dog home at night with him. He also told them his name was Carl and he was a trainee vet. He handed them a card with his name and mobile-phone number on it. Sam, of course, had to give Carl one of his cards too.

'Ring me anytime,' said Carl, 'and I'll let you know how your dog is doing.'

'*Your dog.*' Ella liked that and she could feel tears springing up in her eyes when she had to leave Patch. She noticed Sam saying goodbye in a very shaky voice too.

Outside neither she nor Sam spoke at first. Then Ella remembered something Carl had mentioned. He'd said it was so lucky they'd heard Patch whimpering, and then added, 'You must have very sharp hearing.'

Ella burst out, 'You know, I don't think we'd normally have heard Patch; it's just when we're online —'

'– we've got super hearing as well,' interrupted Sam. 'We're magic, we are.' Then he added a bit more gloomily, 'If only we could find a way to magic ourselves away from the Jolly Roger.'

# Disturbing a Burglar

Uncle Mike and Aunt Joy weren't just angry when Ella and Sam got back, Uncle Mike's lips actually turned white with rage as he bellowed, 'We feed you, put a roof over your heads, and this is how you repay us!'

*All we've done*, thought Ella, *is take a little break from our work on a Saturday afternoon — not robbed a bank or anything.*

'I've never met such ungrateful

children,' screeched Aunt Joy. 'Just looking at you both gives me a headache.'

'Well, we're going to be watching you very carefully in future,' roared Uncle Mike. 'There'll be no more of this going off to play when you feel like it.'

For the rest of the day Sam and Ella were run off their feet. Once they even collided into each other on the stairs. They both giggled until Uncle Mike shouted up, 'Don't waste time laughing!'

The following day – Sunday – was, if anything, even busier. Well, it was for Sam and Ella. Aunt Joy had 'one of her heads' and could only shrill instructions. 'I feel too ill to lift a finger,' she moaned. 'It must be the stress of having such disobedient children to look after.'

Meanwhile, Uncle Mike, frowning furiously, barked orders at Sam and Ella whenever they rushed past.

Ella waited until lunch was over before she asked Aunt Joy if she could go out for just half an hour. She was desperate to see Professor Forbes and find out how much the Roman coin was worth. But Aunt Joy shrieked, 'Don't you know how much work we have to do today? You can't leave here for half a minute.' Then she sank right back in her chair again.

There was just one moment when the twins weren't being watched. That was when two groups of guests swooped down on Uncle Mike and Aunt Joy to complain about a kettle that didn't work and a room that was far too hot.

Ella seized her chance. She rushed into the office. First of all she called Carl to find out how Patch was. To Ella's great relief, Patch was feeling much better and Carl invited them to visit their dog tomorrow.

Then Ella rang Professor Forbes. 'I'm so sorry,' she said, 'but we can't come and see you today.'

'What a pity,' he said, 'for I have some thrilling news for you.'

'Oh, what is it?' she cried.

'I'd rather not tell you on the phone,' said Professor Forbes mysteriously. 'You never know who might be listening in.'

Just then, Sam, who'd been keeping watch, gave two urgent raps on the door. This meant their uncle and aunt were on the way back towards reception.

Ella said quickly, 'Professor, could we come round and see you after school tomorrow?'

'I'll look forward to it,' he replied. 'And please don't worry, I am taking excellent care of your coin. Oh, if you could also remember to bring my glasses . . .?'

In fact, Ella was carrying them around in her pocket just so she didn't forget them. But she had no time to tell him any of this as there was a thunder of thumps on the office door, which meant, 'Leave right now!' So she had to fling the phone down on Professor Forbes rudely before springing out of the office.

She was only just in time as well. For Uncle Mike came striding into reception and would have been furious if he'd known she'd gone into the office – 'out of bounds at all times to kids' – never mind used the phone.

He barked at her, 'What are you doing loitering about here? You haven't a moment to waste.'

At half past five Sam was allowed a half-hour homework break. But Ella wasn't permitted to stop as well. 'You two are as thick as thieves these days,' said Aunt Joy. 'And we think it's best you don't spend so much time together.'

Sam grinned to himself. They couldn't stop him exchanging messages with Ella whenever he wanted. In fact, they'd been chatting online for hours; it was the only thing that had made today bearable.

But when Sam reached his bedroom he received a big shock.

Someone was in Ella's room. He'd left her cleaning the kitchen. And he knew his uncle and aunt were in reception. So who on earth was it?

He listened. Drawers were being opened and things hurled on to the ground. It was obviously a burglar storming about searching for jewels and money. Well, he wouldn't find either of those in Ella's room. No wonder he sounded so angry. Sam could actually hear the burglar snorting with fury.

Sam was burning with rage too. How dare this burglar rifle through his sister's things! He should go in and challenge him. Then he wondered exactly how big the robber was.

A brilliant idea suddenly danced into his head. He'd go online with Ella and become super strong. Then he could charge in there and defeat the burglar, no matter how massive he was. Afterwards he'd be a real hero, wouldn't he? Even Uncle Mike and Aunt Joy would be impressed when they heard how he'd tackled a giant robber, all on his own.

Suddenly the door shot open. A huge man exploded out of it and sped past Sam before he could do anything.

Sam did chase after him, but without his super powers he couldn't run very fast at all. And the only person he bumped into was Uncle Mike, who roared, 'How dare you charge about like a hooligan!'

'A burglar,' panted Sam. 'I just saw one.'

'What are you talking about?' demanded Uncle Mike.

Sam took him to Ella's room.

Uncle Mike looked around him at all the mess and confusion, then stared at Sam through narrowed eyes. 'Some very odd things have been happening here recently,' he said. 'First it's those bent forks, now this phantom burglar.'

'He wasn't a phantom; I saw him.'

'If I find out you're behind this —'

'Me?' exclaimed Sam.

'I wouldn't put anything past you,' said Uncle Mike, breathing very heavily. 'Now clear this mess up. I must check none of the guests' rooms have been disturbed.'

But not one of them had. Only Ella's.

'Do you think,' said Ella, when Sam was helping her to tidy up her bedroom, 'that the robber spotted us on the cliffs finding the coin and now he's after it?'

'Yeah, that must be it,' cried Sam excitedly. 'It proves that coin is worth a fortune. We'll have to take really good care of it when we get it back.' Then he went on, 'I so wish I'd caught that burglar; I never even saw his face. All I can remember about him is that he was very big . . . and his aftershave.'

'His aftershave?' repeated Ella blankly.

'Yeah, I got a real whiff of that. It was

as if he'd had a bath in it: dead strong.
I'll remember if I ever smell it again.'

And Sam did smell it again – the very
next day.

# A Shock
# for Sam

The next day started in a really horrible way – with a maths test. Not Sam's best subject. And he hadn't slept very well so he felt especially awful when he gazed at the paper.

'I shan't get a single mark,' he groaned to himself. Then he knew what to do.

Moments later, Ella heard a buzzing noise in her ear, and then Sam was saying, 'Hey, Ella, be a mate: tell me the answers.'

She was very shocked. 'That's cheating.'

'No, it isn't,' he replied. 'It's helping out your twin brother.'

'It's cheating,' repeated Ella. She added a bit more softly, 'I'm really sorry Sam . . .'

'Oh, go boil your head,' he snapped.


Sam's mood wasn't any better at the end of school. He and Ella were going to look in on Patch at the vet's first, then go and see Professor Forbes. They walked along in total silence. Ella was upset about that. She had really liked it when they'd got on together.

Trying to be friendly, she said, 'Well, I

wonder how much our Roman coin
will be worth?'

'I hope that Professor Forbes hasn't
left the country with it,' said Sam.

Ella laughed. 'He wouldn't do that.'

'He might – or he might substitute
our Roman coin with a fake one.'

'Oh no, Professor Forbes is a famous
archaeologist,' said Ella. 'And he's a very
nice man.'

'I don't think so,' muttered Sam. 'He's
got sly eyes.'

Ella laughed. 'But you can hardly see
his eyes behind those tinted glasses.'

'I can see them,' said Sam. 'And
they're sly.'

'Now you're just being silly.'

'No one knows anything except you,
do they?' said Sam. Then he added

under his breath, 'Miss Goody-Goody.'

They didn't say another word until they reached the vet's.

As soon as Patch saw them, his tail thumped the ground and he stumbled unsteadily over to Sam.

'Look at that,' cried Sam, patting the dog enthusiastically. 'He likes me the best, don't you, boy?'

Ella thought Sam was just being pathetic. And anyway, Patch looked very pleased to see her too.

Carl said he'd done some investigating and was now certain that Patch had been dumped by his previous owner. 'And he's been starving hungry, haven't you, boy?'

Patch wagged his tail.

'Right away he knows we're talking

about him,' said Sam, 'because he's dead clever.' They talked and played with Patch for ages.

At last Ella said, 'I suppose we'd better go and visit Professor Forbes now.'

'You go,' said Sam, 'seeing as you like him so much. I'm staying with Patch for a bit longer.'

Ella was surprised but just said, 'Oh, all right, see you later.'

Sam didn't answer, he just went on playing with Patch. Then, all of a sudden, the dog curled up into a ball and went to sleep.

'He's still quite weak,' explained Carl. 'I expect he'll sleep for a couple of hours now.'

So, after giving Patch a final little pat, Sam left. He decided he'd wait for Ella by Professor Forbes's house. He supposed he hadn't been very nice to her today; well, he knew he hadn't. But she drove him crazy, especially when she acted so perfect.

He was turning into Professor Forbes's road when a large man strode in front of him. And Sam's heart jumped because he thought he could smell that aftershave again. He half ran after the man, and took a huge sniff. Yes, it was him all right. That burglar moved in a cloud of aftershave.

Suddenly the man turned round. He had a beetroot-red face and a thick neck. He stared at Sam for a second. *Perhaps he heard me taking that massive sniff*, thought Sam.

The man marched quickly on again.

Sam hung back a bit. He wanted to trail this guy, see where he went.

But the next moment he received the shock of his life.

He watched the burglar stride confidently down a drive, and then knock on a door. He was let inside at once.

The house belonged to Professor Forbes.

## 'Help!'

Ella had just sat down opposite Professor Forbes – a glass of orange juice and some surprisingly fresh biscuits beside her – when her nose started to itch.

Was this a sneeze, or could it be Sam trying to get through?

The next moment Sam's voice thundered down her ear. 'Grab the coin and get out of there now!'

'But why?' she quavered.

'Just do it,' he ordered. 'Get out now!'
He sounded so serious and urgent, he
really frightened her.

Then she noticed Professor Forbes
looking at her questioningly. He'd
obviously asked her something. 'Sorry,
what was that?'

He smiled. 'I just enquired if you'd
had a hard day at school?'

'Yes, thank you.' Ella was aware that
wasn't quite the right answer, but her
head was spinning. Sam had been so
insistent. Over and over he'd told her to
'Get out now!'

Something really bad must have
happened. She hoped it was nothing to
do with Patch.

She drew a great shuddery breath and

scrambled to her feet. 'Sorry, Professor, but I've just forgotten something. I'll be back in a minute, I expect . . . but could I just take my coin with me?'

Professor Forbes peered at her in some surprise, and then said softly, 'But of course.' He slowly shuffled over to her, the coin in his hand.

Ella snatched it from him, which she really hadn't meant to do, but she was so agitated now. 'I'm sure I'll be back,' she cried.

'Just before you go, my dear,' said Professor Forbes, 'did you happen to bring my glasses with you?'

'I think so,' said Ella, fumbling about in her school bag. She was sure they were in there. But it was overflowing with stuff and her hands were shaking so much that she couldn't seem to find them. 'No, sorry, I must have forgotten them again.'

A look of real disappointment crossed his face but then he said smoothly, 'Well, never mind. Now do look after your coin. We shall have to have our chat about that later.' His voice rose. 'Mrs Saunders, our young friend has got to leave.'

Mrs Saunders bobbed up right away. Ella was sure she'd spent most of her time listening just outside the door. She didn't know why the professor employed someone so creepy.

And at the front door Mrs Saunders snapped, 'The poor professor is totally lost without his glasses.'

'I really thought I'd brought them,'

cried Ella. 'I shan't forget them next time.'

But Mrs Saunders didn't reply. She just stood watching Ella leave, in a very suspicious way.

Out on the pavement Ella bumped straight into Sam. She was out of breath now and very worked up. 'What's happened?' she shrieked.

'Did you just see a man walk in?'

'No,' she replied.

'Well, someone did and I recognized him. It's the guy who tried to rob you.'

'But I thought you didn't see the burglar,' cried Ella.

'I didn't – but I smelt him and especially his rotten aftershave. And that guy in Forbes's house smelt identical . . .'

Ella smiled.

'What's funny?' demanded Sam.

'It's just you gave me the shock of my life and all because . . .'

'I tell you, it's the same person!' Sam was shouting now.

'Loads of people use the same aftershave,' said Ella quietly.

'Not the way he splashes it on, so strong it rots your nose. Actually, I think that guy's working for Professor Forbes.'

'What!' exclaimed Ella in amazement. 'You're saying a famous archaeologist sent a burglar along to my room to steal – well, what exactly? He already had the Roman coin.'

'Did you get it back?' demanded Sam suddenly.

'Yes.'

'Show me,' he cried.

'Oh, honestly,' sighed Ella, digging it out of her pocket. 'Happy now?'

Sam began examining it very carefully. 'You're certain he hasn't switched our coin for a clever fake?'

'I don't think Professor Forbes would do that,' said Ella. 'And I don't believe he sent someone to search my room either.' She picked up her school bag, looked casually inside it, and groaned. 'Oh, there are the professor's glasses,' she cried, waving the case in the air. Then she smiled at Sam and murmured, 'The same aftershave – oh, honestly.'

Sam didn't reply, just looked as if he'd swallowed something very bitter. Then he snatched the case and put the glasses on. 'Oh, give them back,' cried Ella. But

Sam began prancing about in them. Only they were so big they kept falling off his face.

'They're huge,' cried Sam, 'and I can't see a thing through them.'

'That's because you don't need glasses,' said Ella, grabbing them from him. 'And I'll take these before you break them.' She put them back in the case. 'I'm going to pop them back to the professor now – and find out how much our coin –'

'I really don't think you should go back in there,' interrupted Sam.

'Now you're being silly,' said Ella.

'Yes, of course I am,' sneered Sam. 'And what do I know compared to you?'

Ella flushed angrily. 'I just can't talk to you today.'

Without another word she stalked off.

'That's the last time I help her,' muttered Sam. 'She thinks I'm a real turnipbrain anyway.'

But before he reached the Jolly Roger, Sam stopped. A thought had come to him like a thunderclap. Those massive glasses he'd put on, which kept sliding down his face . . . well, Professor Forbes wasn't much bigger than him. So those glasses wouldn't have fitted on his face either!

A shiver ran right through Sam. Those glasses couldn't belong to Professor Forbes at all. But why was he pretending they did? And why did he want them so desperately?

Maybe that was what the burglar had been searching for in Ella's room!

He wondered if he should call Ella and tell her this. He hesitated. And then he heard a deafening shout. It was Uncle Mike yelling at him through the window. 'Stop idling about – and get in here now!'

When he told them Ella had stayed behind at school and would be a bit late, Aunt Joy collapsed in a chair and moaned. 'She thinks she can leave all the work to me. Have you ever known a more ungrateful girl?'

Sam was immediately set to work cleaning the kitchen floor (usually Ella's job). Then he heard the familiar humming noise down his ear. This would be Ella telling him she was on her way back to the Jolly Roger. He waited for her to speak.

But she didn't say a word. And then she was gone.

A few seconds later she called again.

'Ella,' he said at once.

This time she did speak.

She said just one word: 'HELP!'

# Ella in Danger

Only a few minutes earlier Ella had walked confidently up to Professor Forbes's door. It was opened by a stern-faced Mrs Saunders.

'I'm back,' said Ella a little breathlessly. 'You see, I found Professor Forbes's glasses in my bag . . .'

And then Professor Forbes came forward in small, shuffling steps.

'Ah, splendid, I told Mrs Saunders

our young friend would not let me down . . .'

He was interrupted by a very loud banging noise from upstairs. Ella looked up sharply. She could hear someone shouting as well. It sounded like, 'Let me out!'

She saw Professor Forbes and Mrs Saunders exchange tense looks but then he said easily, 'I'm afraid a colleague of mine is not at all well — been overworking. He is resting upstairs but he has these terrible dreams. Mrs Saunders, will you see if you can help the poor chap?' Mrs Saunders raced up the stairs while Ella followed the professor into his sitting room.

'Now do make yourself comfortable, my dear,' he said. 'And I do hope my colleague's bad dreams didn't alarm you unduly.'

'Oh no,' said Ella, but suspicion was growing in her mind now. The professor insisted that Ella have another orange juice and went on being as friendly as possible. But then Mrs Saunders started hoovering right outside the door again. Was that to cover up the noise upstairs? But surely the professor couldn't be involved in anything bad? Or could he?

The professor's whole face lit up when Ella handed him his glasses.

'How I've missed them,' he cried. Then, to Ella's surprise, he called Mrs Saunders. She stopped hoovering and practically ran inside. He gave Mrs Saunders the glasses. 'Will you take them to the shed for me?' He waved airily to a shed which Ella could just make out at the end of the garden. He explained, 'That's where I do most of my research . . . and the glasses are especially useful for close work.'

Then he started talking to Ella about her Roman coin. He said he had wonderful news for her. But when she asked him who the emperor was on her coin, he didn't seem to know. He talked on and on without answering a single one of her questions. Ella was getting more and more suspicious. She took another sip of her drink. And suddenly she wanted to yawn, but that would be terribly rude.

Instead, she announced, 'I think I'll be going now.'

She staggered to her feet. Her legs felt heavy, as if they were made of stone. She was dizzy as well. She clutched the arm of the chair she'd been sitting on. 'I'm sorry,' she began. Then she noticed two other people had come into the room: Mrs Saunders and another man. Could he be the burglar Sam had seen? She peered blearily across at him.

Then everything began to whirl round and round . . .

The next thing she knew, Mrs Saunders was picking her up. She struggled to get out of her grip. 'Professor,' she mumbled, 'what's happening?'

But he didn't answer her, just said to Mrs Saunders, 'She'll be out for at least two hours – plenty of time for us to get away.' And his voice sounded so different

– tougher and much younger. Then she almost lost consciousness, but was dimly aware of being carried upstairs and flung on to a bed.

'She's out all right,' said Mrs Saunders to someone Ella couldn't see. In fact, Ella was still drifting in and out of sleep. And she knew she had to call Sam. But it took every ounce of her concentration. And the first time she heard Sam say, 'Hello,' her head felt so incredibly heavy she couldn't even think.

She tried her hardest to concentrate. This time one word came out with great difficulty: 'Help!'

'Ella, what's happened?' cried Sam.

'Been drugged . . . shouldn't have come back . . . you were right . . . better tell Aunt Joy.'

'No way,' cried Sam. 'I'm coming to get you.'

'You can't,' gasped Ella.

'I bet I can when I'm super strong,' replied Sam. 'But for that to happen I need you to stay awake. The second you fall asleep, all our special powers will vanish.'

'I'll stay awake,' said Ella shakily. 'But when you get there . . . here —' she was getting confused now, '— I mean, what will you do?'

'Don't know exactly,' he said. 'But don't worry, I'll have you out of there very soon — if not sooner.'

Sam sounded really confident but that was a bit of an act for Ella's benefit. Actually, he felt scared and nervous. What could he do?

But then he thought of his sister lying drugged inside that house. And he felt a hot surge of anger. He had to get her out and there wasn't a moment to lose.

Sam squared his shoulders and rapped on Professor Forbes's door.

'I'm going in now, Ella,' he said.

There was no answering voice in his head.

'Ella,' he cried. 'Ella!'

But there was still no reply.

## Who Is in
## the Loft?

*Ella must have fallen asleep,* he
thought. That was terrible. He had
no super powers at all now.

'Ella!' he cried. 'Wake up, please.'

Still no answer.

Then Professor Forbes's door was
pulled open. Sam had been expecting
Mrs Saunders. Instead, this mountain of a
man peered down at him. And he
absolutely stank of aftershave.

'Hello,' said Sam, his voice sounding very squeaky. 'I've come to get my sister, Ella.'

'She's not here,' snapped the man.

'I think she is,' cried Sam, his voice sounding even squeakier.

'She was here about half an hour ago,' admitted the man, 'but she left. You'll find her at home waiting for you.'

Sam knew this was a total lie. In his head he was frantically calling his sister's name. Suddenly his nose started to tickle.

Never had a tickling nose filled Sam with such delight.

Then the buzzing sound filled his head, and Ella's voice, anxious and fearful, came through again. 'Sam, I must have fallen asleep for a few seconds . . . very, very sorry. Where are you?'

'At the door.'

'Oh, be careful,' she cried.

Meanwhile, the man was saying he was very busy and was trying to close the door in Sam's face. But Sam could now feel all this new strength surging through his body. He stopped the door closing and jumped inside.

'What are you doing?' demanded the man. 'Get out!'

'Not without my sister.'

The man lunged at Sam as if to push him out. But then Sam sent his fist flying towards the man. It reached the guy's stomach, where it landed with a crisp, smacking noise.

He gazed at Sam for a moment in total surprise. Then his knees buckled and he fell back.

'You should have seen the punch we just gave him,' cried Sam to Ella. 'And now he's passed out – with shock, I think.'

'Well done,' cried Ella.

'Oh, no one messes with us,' said Sam. 'The house seems to be empty right now,' he went on.

'Yes, I think the professor and Mrs Saunders are both in the shed,' said Ella.

'Excellent. So here I come.'

He bounded up the stairs, and then stopped. 'Ella, I can hear noises coming from the loft.'

And with her new super-hearing powers, Ella could as well. 'I think someone might be trapped up there . . . Be careful, though.'

Sam couldn't see a ladder leading up

to the loft. So, with one bound, he leapt on to the banisters. Then he pushed open the trapdoor and went flying into the loft.

It was dark and gloomy (like all the other rooms in this house) but in one corner was an elderly man tied to a chair. Sam sped over and hastily untied him.

The old man gazed up at Sam. 'I'm extremely grateful to you,' he said. 'Even if I have no idea where you've come from or who you are.'

'I'm Sam and I'll explain the rest later. But we haven't a moment to lose.'

'I understand,' said the man. 'My name, by the way, is Professor Forbes.'

Sam let out a gasp of astonishment. 'So that man downstairs –'

'– is a total impostor,' said Professor Forbes firmly. 'Now, please tell me how to get out of here.'

'Just follow me,' replied Sam, chuffed at the way Professor Forbes saw him as the leader.

He found the loft ladder and let Professor Forbes go down it first. He was telling Ella what had just happened, when Professor Forbes let out a loud groan.

Sam stared down. What he saw filled him with horror.

Three figures had now appeared on the landing: the man he'd sent flying a couple of minutes ago, Mrs Saunders and the fake Professor Forbes – who was brandishing a gun.

## Escape

'D own you come, young man, but very slowly,' ordered the fake Professor Forbes.

Sam obeyed.

'Do not move, either of you,' continued the fake Professor Forbes. He looked much younger now, and had abandoned the tinted glasses. He turned to Sam. 'You are surprisingly strong for your age.' There was a grudging note of approval in his voice.

'He took me by surprise, that's all,' muttered the man, highly embarrassed at having been knocked out by someone a third of his size, and he lumbered up into the loft.

'I'm afraid I must ask you both to follow him,' said the fake professor. 'Then you'll both have to be tied up. But soon we will have gone and I'm sure you will be rescued . . . eventually. Now I insist you follow my instructions immediately.' He waved his gun threateningly.

*That gun changes everything*, thought Sam. He didn't dare risk shots being fired. 'It looks as if we're beaten after all,' he said gloomily to Ella.

Ella opened her eyes and then hauled herself to the door. The fake professor and Mrs Saunders had their backs to her, as they watched the real professor clamber up the steps. They weren't bothered about her, as they assumed she would be asleep for ages yet. And without her super powers Ella would have been.

So here it was. Her chance to escape.

'Sam,' she said, 'I'm going to make a run for it.'

'Too dangerous,' he replied at once.

'No, I think I can do this, if you just keep them talking a bit longer – and stay online, of course.'

Then she heard the fake professor say to Sam – and how sharp and cold his voice now sounded – 'Right, boy, your turn to climb back into the loft.'

'Just before I go,' cried Sam to the fake professor, 'why aren't you wearing your glasses?'

Ella had slowly edged towards the stairs now. She felt quite wobbly with tiredness – and nerves. And suddenly her feet seemed stuck to the floor. She began to tremble. 'No, come on, you can do this,' she said softly to herself. And then she was off, tiptoeing down the stairs just as the fake professor was saying, 'You've no idea, boy, just how important those glasses are. In fact, I'd say they are the most valuable glasses in the world. And please don't think we're not grateful to you and your sister for finding them for us. Of course we are.' He laughed loudly, mockingly.

Mrs Saunders and the man Sam had knocked out joined in.

And then Ella couldn't hear any more, as she was out of the door!

Sam cheered when she told him. 'Now I just need to find the police station,' she said.

Sam was sending her directions but she still got muddled. And in the end she asked a teenage boy. He pointed her in the right direction, and then let out a whistle of astonishment as Ella shot off. 'Faster,' as the boy said afterwards, 'than any Olympic runner.'

Ella fell into the police station, where she started talking so agitatedly the sergeant at the desk told her to take some deep breaths and start again.

This time she told her story to a

policewoman in a small room.
Something Ella said must have impressed
her, because she rushed off. A few
moments later she returned to tell Ella
the police were on their way to
Professor Forbes's house.

Ella looked up at her, smiled, and
promptly fell fast asleep.

# The Most Valuable
# Glasses in the World

Four days later, Ella, Sam and
Professor Forbes were having their
picture taken outside the Jolly Roger.

'That's perfect,' began the
photographer. But then Uncle Mike
blundered right in front of them.

'Could I ask everyone to move back
slightly, so we can get the Jolly Roger
sign into the picture as well? Thank you
all so much.'

After the picture was taken, Uncle Mike gave a revolting smile, showing off all his brown teeth. He turned to the reporter and said, 'You might add that we offer a warm welcome here every single day and have special weekend rates.'

'Yes, sir,' murmured the reporter. She was quite new at doing this but she knew a pompous windbag when she saw one.

She went over to the professor. 'You've been through an awful experience,' she said.

'I certainly have,' he said. 'Imprisoned in my own house for nearly a week, while criminals stole my good name.'

'And would you just explain to our readers exactly why they did that?' asked the reporter.

'No, I won't, actually,' he replied. 'I shall leave that to my new young friends.' He beamed at Ella and Sam. He'd visited them every day since they'd rescued him. And now they both felt very at ease with him. 'So who would like to start?'

'You can,' hissed Sam to Ella.

So she gave a nervous little cough and then began.

'Earlier this year the biggest jewel robbery for ages took place. It was committed by just one man — an international jewel thief called Anton Korski. He's clever and cunning, but he needed a gang to help him get the jewels out of the country. And he didn't dare write down the secret information that revealed where the jewels were hidden. Instead, he had some glasses made up with a very special prescription.'

Ella turned to Sam. 'You tell the next bit.'

'Once his glasses were found,' said Sam eagerly, 'you just had to work out the prescription – and by the way, Mrs Saunders had once been an optician – because hidden in that prescription was a secret code –'

'Giving the exact map reference where the jewels could be found!' exclaimed the reporter.

'That's right,' said Sam. 'He was going to hand over the glasses to the gang on the cliffs. But then he saw the police closing in on him so he buried the glasses – just before he was captured.

Ella and I saw him being captured, by the way,' Sam added, with a little swagger. Then he continued with his explanation. 'So the gang knew he'd buried the glasses out on the cliffs, but hadn't a clue where. The gang were also being watched by the police so, if they started a big search there, they would arouse suspicions right away. They needed a cover story. You tell the last bit, Ella.'

'So then,' said Ella excitedly, 'they heard about the rare Roman coin found on the cliffs and how this local archaeologist – who hardly anyone ever saw – had begun searching for more coins. Well, that gave them the perfect cover. One of the gang members even looked a little like the professor.'

'A very little,' said Professor Forbes with a shudder.

'He pretended to be the professor, although he was careful not to be seen too closely – that's why the house was always so dark. Meanwhile, the gang let on they were working for the professor, searching for rare coins, when of course they were looking for something quite different – which we discovered.'

'I'm only sorry,' said Professor Forbes, 'the fake me pretended that the coin you found, featuring the noble portrait of Augustus, was worth a great deal of money. It is worth about seventy-five pounds though –'

'Which isn't bad,' cut in Sam.

'No,' agreed the professor. 'And I shall make sure you both receive that.' He glanced sharply at Uncle Mike and Aunt Joy, as if to say, 'And don't you two try and take it.'

Then he turned to Sam and Ella again. 'And now I have one last surprise for you.'

## Professor Forbes's Incredible Surprise

The reporter, who'd been scribbling furiously, looked up, and Ella and Sam wondered what the professor was doing.

Professor Forbes gave a little signal and then, walking towards them came Carl, with Patch squirming excitedly in his arms. Carl let Patch go and the dog dived over to Ella and Sam, going absolutely wild with joy at the sight of them both.

'Patch, how are you?' cried Sam, patting him as if he was never going to stop.

'These marvellous children haven't just rescued an old duffer like me,' said Professor Forbes. 'They also saved this dog, which was in a very bad way when they found him. No one's come forward to claim the poor creature and Ella and Sam have visited him every day –' Aunt Joy gave a gasp of surprise at this news – 'and I know they would like to look after Patch for good.' He turned to Uncle Mike and Aunt Joy. 'That is, if you have no objection?'

Uncle Mike's face went all twisted up like a cat's bottom, while Aunt Joy gave another, even louder, gasp. Of course they had objections: tons and tons of them.

'I'm sure you wouldn't deny these brave children their own dog,' went on Professor Forbes. 'I think they deserve that, don't you?' He was staring intently at Uncle Mike now. And so were the reporter, the photographer and Carl.

Uncle Mike gulped very hard and even managed to conjure up a tiny smile. 'No, of course you can keep this mutt . . . I mean, delightful dog.'

Professor Forbes shot a look of triumph at the twins. Only yesterday they had confided in him how much they wanted to look after Patch, but they feared their uncle and aunt would never agree. The professor had known exactly how to get round that.

Ella hugged Patch in delight. 'Isn't it great, you're going to live with us forever.'

Just before leaving, the professor presented them with a lead and collar for Patch. He said, 'I hope you'll allow me to visit you two, and Patch, from time to time.'

'But of course,' cried Ella and Sam together.

'Up to now I have just lived for my work,' he said. 'But this little adventure has made me realize there are other important things in life too.'

After he'd gone, Uncle Mike insisted the reporter and photographer take some pictures of Ella and Sam's 'happy home', while Aunt Joy cooed, 'And you two dear children can just go off and play.'

The 'dear children' nearly fell over with shock. As they walked away, Sam said to

Ella shyly, 'This has been a wicked day. And I'm glad we're talking again.'

'So am I,' agreed Ella at once. And happiness just exploded inside her head like fireworks.

'I think,' Sam went on, 'we shouldn't use our special powers for things like cheating,' he blushed slightly, 'but to rescue lots more animals . . . and the odd person.'

'And to solve more mysteries,' cut in Ella keenly.

'Oh yeah, we'll definitely do that.' A slow smile spread across his face. 'It's going to be so great.'

Sam, Ella and Patch walked along together in the dancing sunlight.

Then they tore down on to the beach, eager to start their next adventure.

Crime-busting action from 2 kids with super powers!

2 POWER

Sam and Ella, the crime-busting duo, will return in summer 2007 with their second action-packed adventure: *The Canine Conspiracy.*